Cuddle Up, Goodnight

Katie Cleminson

Disney • Hyperion Books • New York

For Bee and Bird

Text and illustrations copyright © 2010 by Katie Cleminson
First published under the title *Wake Up!* in Great Britain in 2010 by Random House UK

This book is set in P22Garamouche.
The art was created using inks, colored pencil, and charcoal.
First U.S. edition, 2011
1 3 5 7 9 10 8 6 4 2
F383-2370-2-10288
Printed in China
Reinforced binding
Library of Congress Cataloging-in-Publication Data on file.
ISBN 978-1-4231-3844-0
Visit www.disneyhyperionbooks.com

It's time to wake up . . .

and start the day

with friends!

Time to stretch and scratch,

clean and rub,

brush that hair,

give teeth a scrub.

It's time to dress up!

Find pants and tees,

shoes and socks,

shorts and coats,
and favorite tops.

Pull and zip,   and tie a bow,

add a hat—

now, off you go!

It's time to
listen up!

Read and draw,

count and spell,

$$11 \quad 9 \quad \% \quad \frac{2 \quad 4 \quad - \quad 7}{3 \quad + \quad 5 \quad X}$$
$$12 \quad 14 \quad \div \quad 13$$
$$10 \quad 6$$

ask and answer,

show and tell.

and up,

It's time to swing up,

and up!

Run and jump,   climb and slide,

sing and dance,   seek and hide.

It's time
to eat up!

Chew and sip,

slurp and crunch,

use knife and fork,

chomp and munch.

It's time to clean up!

Then pick and choose,
search and look,

and read aloud
the perfect book.

At last it's time to . . .

Cuddle up!

yawn and stretch,

Say goodnight,

close your eyes,

sleep and rest . . .

Rest up for another day
with friends!